The Pizza Tree

Published in the United States by 'N Gratitude Publishing Company

Atlanta, Georgia

www.NGratitude.net

ISBN 978-0-9833150-8-7

Printed in the United States of America

Paperback

The Pizza Tree

To Aubrey,
Readers are leaders
and leaders are smart!
Willa Brigham
12·15

Written by Willa Brigham

Illustrated by Mone Bell-Arrington

This book is dedicated to my wonderful spouse, Lovey;

to our sons, Jason and Jarett;

our grandchildren, Jeremih, Jayda and Davonte;

my mother, Louise W. Nall;

and to my brothers, Felix, Jonas, Billy and WR.

Odetta's Grand Papa loved to travel. He was introduced to travel when he was in the Navy and he wanted to visit all seven continents.

"Living in Alabama is all right, but see as much of the world as you can. It is a beautiful place," he would say. Grand Papa sent Odetta gifts from many of the countries he visited.

Shortly after breakfast, the mailman delivered to Odetta an emerald green envelope stamped with sparkling butterflies. It was her special letter from Grand Papa. 'What would this gift be?' Odetta thought to herself.

From Switzerland, she received sweet dark chocolates. From India, Grand Papa sent her beautiful matching bracelets of gold and emerald. She received skirts and blouses from Brazil; and from Egypt, shoes covered in camel hair. But today's gift was totally different.

Slowly she opened the envelope and out dropped the most peculiar object — a small star-shaped item with brilliant colors: brick house red, marigold yellow, olive black, marshmallow white, eggplant purple, pepper green and periwinkle blue.

This was most unusual!

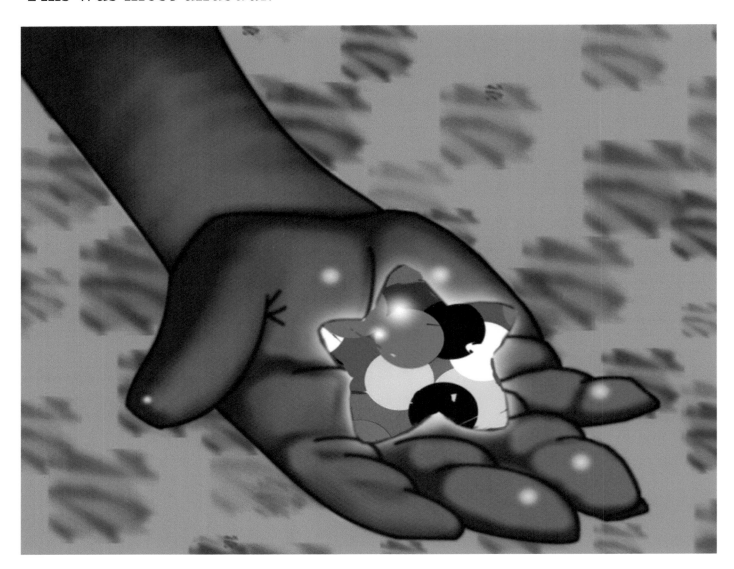

"Oh my! " Odetta exclaimed. "This is the most beautiful object I have ever seen. But what is it?"

A note was included: *"This seed is supposed to have magical powers but I have no idea what they are. It was given to me by a fisherman. It came out of the belly of a fish! Dig a hole in the ground and plant the seed. The sun will come out, the rain will come down, and the seed will grow."*

In the garden, Odetta and her mom chose a spot between the tomato vines and the blueberry bushes, the perfect sunny spot for the seed. They were not sure if it would be a bush or tree and they wanted it to have plenty of room to grow.

A week later, when Odetta was gathering raspberries and cucumbers she noticed the tiny tree. The magical seed had sprouted several branches and pea green leaves had begun to appear. But something was very very different. A familiar smell tickled her nose as she bent to sniff the leaves.

"Mom!" yelled Odetta. "This tree smells strange."

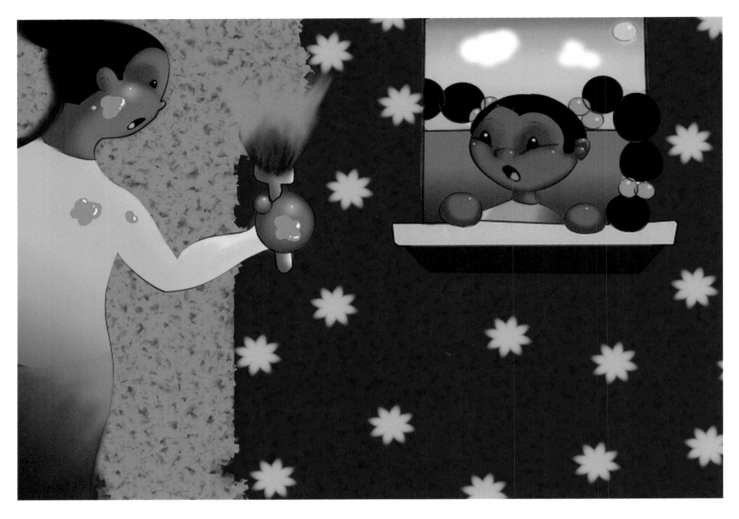

"What does it smell like?" asked Mom, peeping through the window. She was painting the wall in the kitchen.

"It smells like cheese!" said Odetta.

"Trees do not smell like cheese," Mom replied, laughing at the thought.

"This one does," Odetta answered.

"Okay," said Mom. "I will come out when I finish this wall."

But Mom did not come. The phone rang and she forgot all about the tree, and so did Odetta.

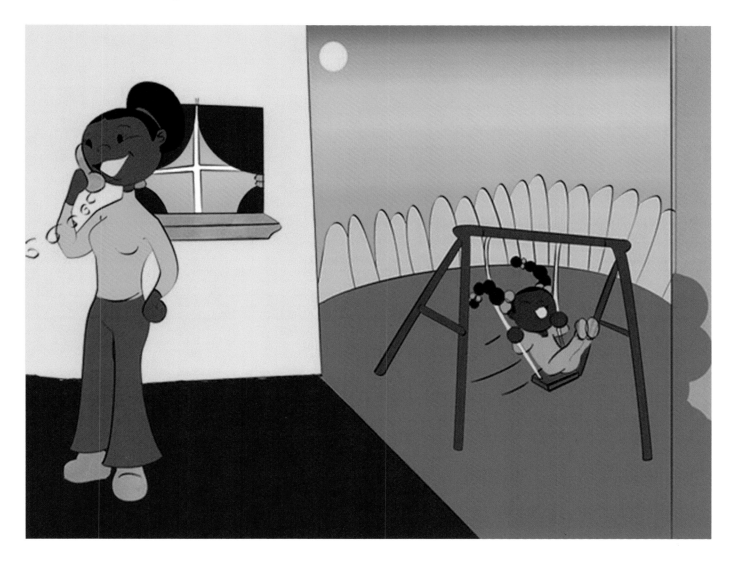

Days later Odetta went out to the garden, her favorite place to be. She was picking sweet peas for cooking and fresh flowers for the dinner table. She loved daisies and had chosen several bright orange ones when she noticed the tree. The tree had grown 12 inches — a whole foot!! To make things more interesting, a familiar smell filled the air. She sniffed!

"Mom!" yelled Odetta standing near the tree. "This tree smells strange."

""What does it smell like today?" asked Mom. She was in the garage changing the tire on her bicycle.

"It smells like baking bread," Odetta answered.

"Baking bread?" questioned Mom. "Is it wheat bread or white bread?"

"Odetta, I don't think trees smell like bread," said Mom.

"This one does!" stated Odetta, giving the tree another sniff. "I will be there in a bit," Mom replied.

Mom examined the tree but could not smell anything. Her allergies had her nose stuffed up.

Mom finished repairing her bicycle and wanted to take a ride before the sun went down. She invited Odetta to ride with her.

Off they rode to the park, forgetting about the tree that smelled like baking bread.

Later, Odetta was in the garden picking sweet juicy blueberries. She and Mom were going to bake a cobbler for dessert. Odetta ate as many as she picked because they were so yummy.

As she reached for berries high up in the branches her nose began to tickle. The smell was very familiar!

"Mom!" called Odetta. "You won't believe this!"

"What is it my dear?" asked Mom. She had both hands in a bucket of soapy water while washing the family car.

"It's the tree. It smells strange!" said Odetta.

"What does it smell like this time?" asked Mom.

"It smells like pepperoni! You need to come and smell it now!" called Odetta.

Mom dropped the sponge into the bucket and ran toward the garden. Odetta stood near the tree and watched as the most amazing thing happened. The tree began to pop, pop, pop. Just like popcorn. With each pop little flowers burst open and the smell of cheese, baking bread, and pepperoni filled the whole garden.

"Wow!" said Odetta.

"Amazing!" said Mom.

Mom looked at the flowers not believing what she was seeing. The flowers had the same colors as the seed: brick house red, marigold yellow, olive black, marshmallow white, eggplant purple, pepper green, and periwinkle blue. Mom slowly pulled the petals away and in the middle of each flower was a "miniature pizza."

"Ohhh my goodness! It is a pizza tree, a pizza tree. Growing in the garden is a pizza tree," sang Odetta, laughing with joy.

"A pizza tree," echoed Mom. "Oh my goodness!"

They each pulled a flower from the tree and cautiously looked it over. Next, they both sniffed and took a bite. It was delicious!! Low fat cheese, pepperoni, and fresh veggies on a thin crust.

"How can this be?" asked Mom.

"Grand Papa said it was a magic seed," replied Odetta.

"Amazing," said Mom, as she took another delicious bite.

"What are we going to do with all of this pizza?"

Odetta thought about that question. It didn't take long for her to come up with a big idea.

"Why don't we invite our neighbors to a pizza party?" asked Odetta

"Good idea," replied Mom.

All the neighbors came and picked fresh pizza from the tree. It was wonderful! They danced, sang, and ate a lot of pizza. Everyone had questions about that tree.

Their neighbors remembered their manners and helped with the clean-up. Each of them thanked Odetta and her mom for the invitation to dinner, and they all went home full and happy.

The Pizza Tree was the talk of the community!

A few weeks later after a morning rain shower, Odetta was in the garden picking green beans when she smelled something familiar. Immediately, she ran toward the Pizza Tree and was met with a wonderful surprise.

"Mom!" she yelled. "It is happening again!"

Mom left the can of paint sitting near the half-painted flowerpots. She arrived to see the explosion of color. The tree was in full bloom, popping like popcorn.

"Pop, pop, pop!"

The popping was so loud that it sounded like fireworks on the Fourth of July. Each flower was more brilliant than the next. Brick house red, marigold yellow, olive black, marshmallow white, eggplant purple, pepper green and periwinkle blue! Once again, each blossom held a miniature pizza.

The smell of fresh baked pizza filled the backyard.

"Oh dear," said Mom. "What are we going to do with all of the pizza this time?"

"Well," said Odetta, as the flower-filled pizzas covered the tree. "I saw some people standing in line at the food bank. Many of them do not have enough food to eat. Let's invite all of them to eat from the Pizza Tree!"

"Great idea," said Mom.

They had many guests for lunch and they all ate from the Pizza Tree. Odetta told the story of how the Pizza Tree came to be, and all were amazed.

It was not long before all the pizza was gone. After lunch, each guest was happy to help with the clean-up. Everyone left with happy stories and smiles of thankfulness.

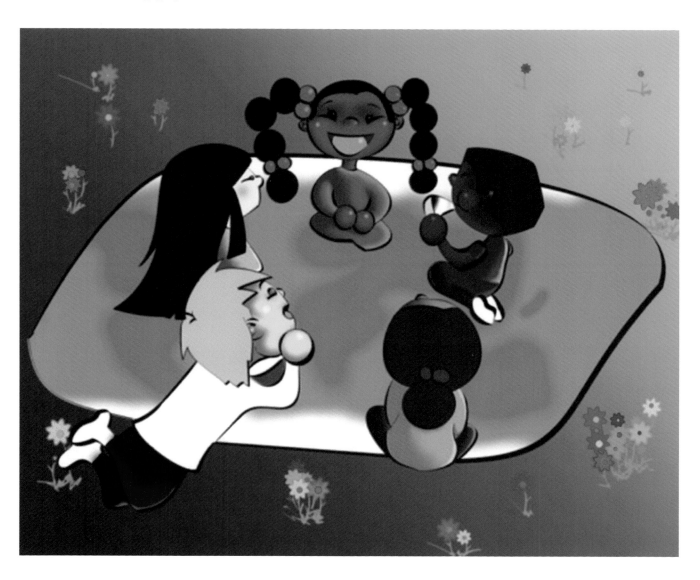

Summer was almost over and the garden had produced a bounty of fresh vegetables. There were crisp greens, sweet onions, cucumbers, blueberries, raspberries, tomatoes, and sweet peppers.

Odetta was picking the last of the sweet juicy cherries from a tree when the smell of fresh baked pizza drifted through the air. She quickly turned from the cherries and raced for the Pizza Tree.

It had been several weeks since the last pizza popping.

"Pop, Pop, Pop!" Was the sound coming from the tree?

"Mom," called Odetta. "Come quickly!"

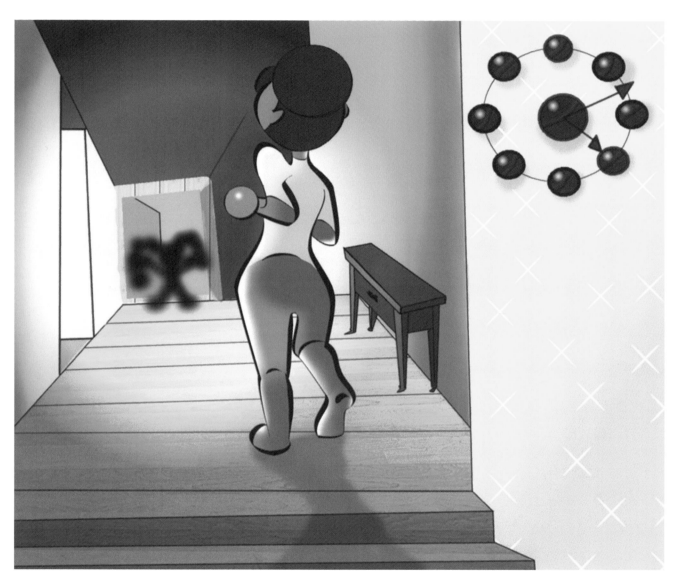

"Can you believe this?" she asked, shaking her head.

"Amazing!" said Mom. Just as she reached the tree the popping stopped.

This time there were no colorful flowers or delicious pizza. Instead, they were face to face with hundreds of seeds. Star shaped with seven brilliant colors: brick house red, marigold yellow, olive black, mushroom white, eggplant purple, pepper green, and periwinkle blue.

Looking at them Mom asked, "What are we going to do with all of these seeds?"

"Well, I have heard of whole countries where people do not have enough food to eat, Odetta answered. "Why don't we send them some seeds with the note Grand Papa sent me? If everyone plants a tree, there will be food enough for everyone."

"Good idea," said Mom. "But who is going to mail all of those letters?"

"We could ask our neighbors and anyone who ate from the Pizza Tree to help," said Odetta.

"I bet they would be happy to send out a few letters."

In the spring, Odetta received hundreds of letters written by people from all over the world. The letters told of their good fortune to have received such a seed from Odetta. Because of her generosity, people in their county were no longer hungry.

And one bright sunny day, Odetta opened the door to a very happy surprise. It was Grand Papa! He was home from his travels and he had stopped in for a visit.

Odetta gave him a big hug. She could not wait to tell him the story of the magical seed and the amazing Pizza Tree!

About the Author

In addition to having a passion for writing children's books, Willa Brigham is an entertaining storyteller, performing artist, inspirational speaker, avid quilter, and television host.

Her work in television has earned her 2 Emmy Awards (5 nominations) in the category of **Best Educational Programming for Young Children.** Willa's passion for education, celebrating diversity, and her knack for adding a bit of zany in her art expression has inspired her to write her latest book, *The Pizza Tree.*

Willa has been recognized as a Woman of Distinction by the North Carolina Federation of Women. She is a member of the National Speakers Association (NSA), National Association of Black Storytellers (NCABS); and with her funloving side not going unnoticed, a Toastmasters Humorous Contest winner.

She has an earlier published book called, *Golden Years* – a humorous look at seniors enjoying their senior years. Her 6 recorded CD's for children (music and stories) include: *Healthy Happy Habits, Something Good, Willa Will,* and *Stinky Johnson.* She has also released 2 adult CD's: What *You See* and *Midnight Quilter.*

Willa has lived in Cary, North Carolina for the past 21 years with her husband Ron and the couple recently celebrated their 40th wedding anniversary. She is a mother of two and grandmother of three.

CPSIA information can be obtained
at www.ICGtesting.com
Printed in the USA
BVIC01n1557181115
427558BV00001B/1